Pizazz

IT'S NOT EASY BEING SUPER...

COMING SOON . . .

PiZAZZ
vs
THE NEW KID

PIZAZZ

IT'S NOT EASY BEING SUPER...

Sophy Henn

SIMON & SCHUSTER

First published in Great Britain in 2020 by Simon & Schuster UK Ltd

Text and Illustrations copyright © 2020 Sophy Henn

1 3 5 7 9 10 8 6 4 2

Simon & Schuster UK Ltd
1st Floor, 222 Gray's Inn Road
London
WC1X 8HB

www.simonandschuster.co.uk

Simon & Schuster Australia, Sydney
Simon & Schuster India, New Delhi

A CIP catalogue record for this book is available from the British Library.

PB ISBN 978-1-4711-9398-9
eBook ISBN 978-1-4711-9399-6

Printed and bound by CPI Group (UK) Ltd, Croydon, CR0 4YY

MIX
Paper from
responsible sources
FSC® C020471
FSC
www.fsc.org

The bit about me...

OK. Well, I am 9¼, almost 9½ and my name is **PIZAZZ**.

Yes, you did hear that right. My name is

PIZAZZ.

And yes, it IS completely embarrassing. And no, I don't think it's a proper name either, but as with most things around here it really doesn't seem to matter what I think about it.

With a ridiculous name like **PIZAZZ** I should probably be a **magician**, or a **POP STAR**, or a **really smelly perfume**, but I am not any of those things.

What I actually am is super. Not super as in brilliant, or terrific or even very good. I am **SUPER** super. *Actually* super. As in superhero, with powers and stuff.

Because of this, I HAVE to wear a costume and part of that costume is a very annoying cape. It gets in the way, flapping around my feet and trailing in puddles and getting stuck in doors, but I still have to wear it

ALL THE TIME.

Not just when it's cold.

. . . And my ridiculous name (which in case you hadn't already guessed I **HATE**) is written right across the back of my cape in **HUGE** shiny letters.

SUPER.

I come from a family of **SUPERHEROES**, which is generally how it works. Not always, I mean, there's the occasional freak accident in a scientist's lab or a weird weather/insect/reclusive millionaire 'incident' that ends up with a perfectly normal person being able to climb up glass buildings or make lightning or jump really, really, really high or suddenly talk in a low gravelly voice. But mainly you're just born and find yourself in a family of **SUPERHEROES** and you can fly and stuff. Then if you are like me you might find yourself wondering why you don't feel quite as delighted about this as the rest of your family does.

MY *SUPER* FAMILY

The most annoying person in my family is definitely my little sister. She's like a **SUPERHERO** crossed with a **CHEERLEADER** crossed with someone who is completely good at everything. Oh, and did I mention she's really happy all the time? Well, she is.

Also, unlike me, she's actually got a cool superhero name . . . RED DRAGON.

Which is just ANOTHER of the many reasons I know my parents prefer her to me.

FIRST DAY AT NURSERY...

THE MOLECULAR STRUCTURE OF CHOCOLATE

A HOUSE

FIRST SCHOOL SPORTS DAY...

ON YOUR MARKS, GET SET...   GOOOOOOOOOOOO...   ...OH.

FIRST SCHOOL PLAY...

AUDITIONS

CAST LIST

ME

SEE WHAT I MEAN?

I call her **RED** for short because **RED DRAGON** is quite a mouthful to say if you just want someone to pass the TV remote, get a snack or even GO AWAY. But she is absolutely **NOT** allowed to call me **PIZZ**. If I am feeling generous she can call me **ZAZZ**, but she is never really sure when I am actually feeling generous, and if I am honest neither am I, so she tends to just call me **PIZAZZ**. With a name like **RED DRAGON** obviously her super power is that she can breathe **fire**, which is really useful not just for defeating baddies but at barbecues, too, and for birthday cake candles. She's also got **SUPER SPEED**, which is OK, I suppose. They are all way cooler than my super power which is the least cool of all the super powers, and in fact so uncool that sometimes I even consider letting the baddies win so I don't actually have to use it. Yes, it's THAT embarrassing. Anyway, I cannot even talk about it right now.

It's just all **SO** unfair.

BEFORE . . .

My parents were sort of super famous about a million years ago because they have saved the word about a trillion times, but these days they just make me and RED do everything. Neutralise rockets, realign planets, load the dishwasher. It's like we are their personal servants or something.

And if you think it's hard to have your **mum** and **dad** cheering you on from the sidelines at sports day, try having them cheer you on while you and your irritating little sister divert a **planet-sized** meteor that's on a direct collision course with Earth. Yup. No pressure.

And, unlucky for me, it's not just my immediate family that are completely weird. Oh no. It's actually my entire family . . .

Uncle Teaser
(Mum's little brother)

Uncle Titanooooooo
(Dad's little brother and yes, there are that many 'o's)

Grandma
(Mum's mum)

Gramps
(Mum's dad)

Red Dragon
(Annoying)

Mum

Me dub

Dad

Grandmother
(Dad's slightly scary mum)

Aunty Fury
(Dad's sister who went to the dark side ... We don't talk about her much)

Wanda
(Not a pet)

Aunty Blaze
(Dad's AWESOME sister)

We have a dog. She's not exactly a pet dog, but more like a total bossy boots who happens to have four legs, a tail, flappy ears and can't resist running after anything you throw. We call her **WANDA**, because that's her name, and she came to us from **MISSION CONTROL** who are basically in charge of which super goes where, saves what and when. So, instead of having an actual phone to talk to **MISSION CONTROL** like normal, sensible people, we have a dog who receives and transmits messages and generally keeps an eye on us. Although totally embarrassing and completely weird, it does actually work OK most of the time, though **WANDA** is absolutely **NOT** allowed to go on any missions any more. This is because Dad threw one of **DABOMB**'s **super scratchy itching powder bombs** into outer space just before it exploded, but **WANDA** *zoomed off* and fetched it right back just in time for it to explode and make us all **itch** FOR EVER. (Well, not quite for ever, but at least a month.)

ROCKET

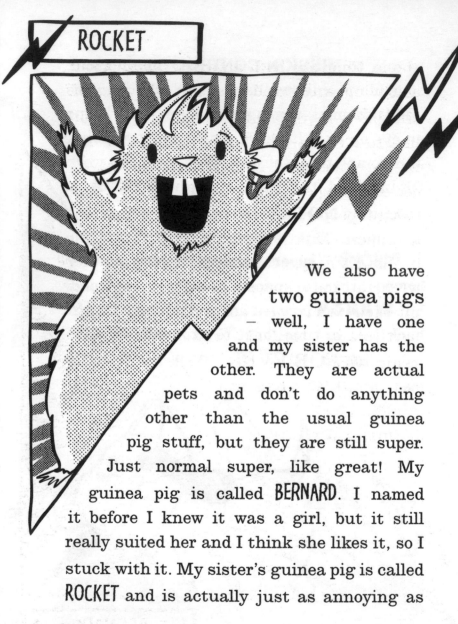

We also have **two guinea pigs** – well, I have one and my sister has the other. They are actual pets and don't do anything other than the usual guinea pig stuff, but they are still super. Just normal super, like great! My guinea pig is called BERNARD. I named it before I knew it was a girl, but it still really suited her and I think she likes it, so I stuck with it. My sister's guinea pig is called ROCKET and is actually just as annoying as she is. They are both always *dashing* about, achieving stuff and basically showing off. BERNARD is more laid-back, like me. We both like to sleep a lot and eat a lot, too. And we have the same favourite snack: prawn-cocktail crisps. Nice.

Most people seem to think that being a superhero must be completely brilliant. They are actually very wrong. You have probably guessed that I am not particularly thrilled with being **SUPER**, BUT there are a FEW good things about it. Just a few.

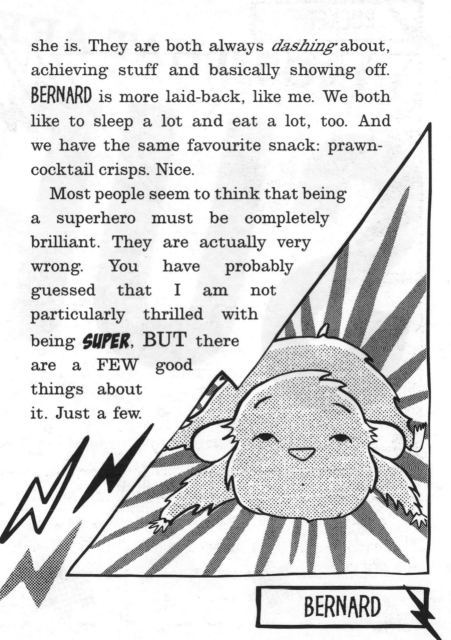

BERNARD

THINGS THAT ARE
SUP

① FLYING...

Obviously that is a great thing, *but not all superheroes can actually fly, i.e. my little sister. HAHAHAHAHAAAAAAA.

* I mean . . . FLYING!

2 HAVING A WHOLE FAMILY OF SUPERHEROES WHO ARE WATCHING OUT FOR YOU...

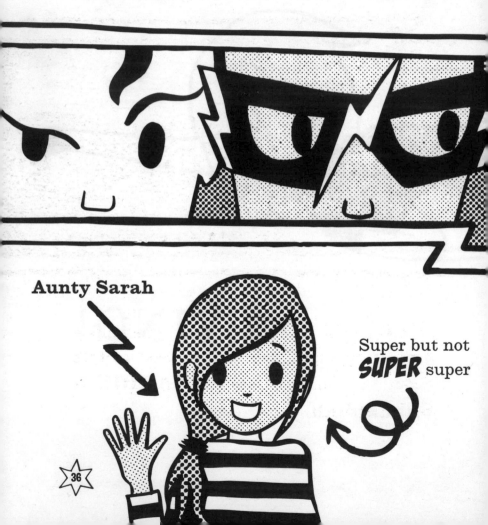

Aunty Sarah

Super but not **SUPER** super

Well, I say a whole family, but there is my Aunty Sarah and she's not actually a superhero. Well, not in the usual sense, though my **mum** says she should have a medal for putting up with my *Uncle Teaser*.

She has a point. And then there's my *Aunty Fury* who I am not supposed to talk about as she is now a **BADDIE!!!** **Shhhhhhh.**

☾ YOU GET SUPER POWERS ...

This is normally a great thing, especially if your power is like

SUPER SPEED

OR

SUPERSTRENGTH

OR LASER EYES

. . . that can see through people and even buildings. But if you are me and have the worst most awful **embarrassing** *SUPER POWER* in the universe then it definitely belongs on the next list . . .

NOT SO SUPER...

There are waaaaaaaay more **RUBBISH** things about being a superhero. At least I think so . . .

① SCHOOL ...

Even though I am a **SUPERHERO**, *whizzing* around saving a world or a town or a kitten from almost certain doom, I still have to go to school, which seems a bit much to me. **Mum** is ALWAYS **blah, blah, blahing** about how it's important to have something to fall back on just in case all the baddies decide to turn over a new leaf. As if! As far as I can work out, no matter how many baddies get defeated, there are just a million more queueing up behind them to cause havoc with their fancy *LASER* blasters and snazzy **STINK-BOMB** makers.

❷ YOU HAVE TO WEAR THE SAME OUTFIT THE WHOLE TIME ...

Well, we have lots of spares of the same outfit. I mean, we're not gross. Apart from **FARTERELLA** – **she really is gross** – but other than that we are actually fairly hygienic.

3 YOU ARE ALWAYS DISAPPEARING OFF TO SAVE ALL OF MANKIND...

One minute you are about to choose a delicious ice cream – *will it be banana-chocolate chip or toffee-chocolate chip or chocolate-chocolate chip?* – and the next minute you're zooming off on a mission. It can **REALLY** get in the way of stuff and not just delicious ice creams.

Here are some examples of just how annoying it can be . . .

EXAMPLE 3

A WICKED GENIUS HAS MADE A GIANT STINK BOMB AND IS THREATENING TO EXPLODE IT ALL OVER THE QUEEN'S BIRTHDAY PARTY, AND INSTEAD OF GOING BOWLING FOR YOUR FRIEND'S BIRTHDAY LIKE YOU WERE SUPPOSED TO, YOU IN ACTUAL FACT HAVE TO SPEND THE WHOLE AFTERNOON THWARTING THE WICKED GENIUS'S EVIL PLANS...

AND GETTING SOAKED IN STINK JUICE...

...WHICH TAKES THREE WEEKS TO PROPERLY WASH OUT.
PEEEUUUUUWWWWW!

4 ALL THAT DISAPPEARING MAKES IT REALLY HARD TO HAVE FRIENDS...

Despite this I did actually have two of the best friends in the whole world, universe even, **Tom** and **Susie**, at my old school. They never ever, ever got annoyed with me constantly disappearing. They never thought my cape was strange and they didn't even mind about the **STINK JUICE**. I guess that's because I have known them my whole life and that's how things have always been – they were used to having a superhero best friend. Called **PIZAZZ**.

But now everything's changed because besides giving me the worst name ever AND a stupid cape, my parents decided they needed to **ruin my life** a bit more by making us move house. In fact, not just house, but to a whole new town, which is hard enough normally, but when you are a **super weirdo** like me I am certain it is even harder. There's just so much to explain all the time. Maybe I should just get it all printed on a T-shirt. Or a cape. **Ha. Ha.**

AND THEN THERE'S . . .

5

YOU ALWAYS HAVE TO BE THE GOODIE, even when you don't feel like it.

6

THE WHOLE OF EARTH'S EXISTENCE DEPENDS ON YOU. Well, not JUST you, you and all the other superheroes . . . but sometimes just you if the others are busy with something else. And that can be quite a worry.

7

YOU SPEND A LOT OF YOUR TIME WISHING YOU WERE NORMAL. Well, at least I do.

2

The bit where I start a
new school...

The new place we live isn't SOOOOOOOO bad. It's just not the old place, which was, and always will be, the BEST place. Also I have no friends. Even after living here for three whole months.

I rang **Susie** this evening. We talked and she told me everything that was happening at my old school, and it was really nice to hear about everyone, but then she had to go as it was **ROLLER DISCO** night and **Tom** called by for her while we were on the phone. I know if I was there I would have gone too and I really don't want to feel jealous because I love them both. But I'm not, so I didn't. And I did feel jealous. I asked **Mum** if I could fly over for a couple of laps, but she said only if I had done all my homework, which I obviously hadn't as I had been on the phone to **Susie**.

I miss them.

And **ROLLER DISCOS**.

Everything wouldn't be quite so bad at my new school if **Mrs Harris** hadn't made one of '**The Populars**' be my 'buddy' – you know, the person who looks after you and shows you around when you are new in school and have NO FRIENDS.

The other one

Serena

The other, other one

You didn't need super vision to see **Serena** pull a puking face when **Mrs Harris** picked her to be my buddy. It's completely humiliating following her around the whole time and knowing that she and the rest of **The Populars** would rather I just disappear.

And how am I supposed to be all friend-makingly funny and witty when I get dragged out in the middle of the night to go on **SUPER** missions?

Hmmmmmm?

WAKEY WAKEY!

SUPER EVIL BADDIE AND GENERAL BOTHER **LAZERDROME** HAS DECIDED TO LAUNCH AN ATTACK ON PLANET EARTH IN THE MIDDLE OF THE NIGHT BECAUSE HE DOES NOT CARE THAT THERE IS SCHOOL TOMORROW...

OUR HEROES ZOOM OUT TO LAZERDROME'S VOLCANIC HQ.

We got home at six a.m. and I still had to go to school, which was completely **UNFAIR**. **Mum** said we would be fine if we had a nap. A nap? Aren't they for babies or old people or **dads** on Sundays? As I am none of those I decided I would **NOT** nap. That'll show **Mum**.

AFTER SCHOOL . . .

So. Tired. I was so completely exhausted and so happy to get home from school, especially because I accidentally fell asleep in physics and dribbled a bit on the desk and now **Serena** hates me more than ever. I was just lying on my bed enjoying staring at the ceiling when **RED** burst in to tell me we were leaving in ten minutes for **Grandma** and **Gramps**'s house. Helpfully, rolling off the bed and hitting the floor woke me up a bit.

THUD!

We live near **Grandma** and **Gramps** now, and they are the main reason my life has been turned upside down and basically RUINED. **Mum** wanted us to live closer to them so we can help out more as they are really old. I tried to argue that if we can all fly halfway round the world in under a minute to redirect a baddie's rocket into deep space, then popping over to help **Gramps** lift a car or something should be no problemo. Unsurprisingly **Mum** wasn't listening though. But if I have to ruin my life for anyone I suppose I am glad it is them.

Grandma and **Gramps** are retired from being **SUPERHEROES** now and I don't think **Grandma** misses it one bit, but **Gramps** always likes to know what's been happening. What I like best about **Gramps** is that, like **RED**, one of his super powers is making fire, from nowhere, out of nothing. He still does it from time to time, but mainly by accident. All you have to do is make him laugh so hard he does a little trump and that comes out as a ~~tiny fireball~~. It is HILARIOUS!

Only **Grandma** doesn't think so as they have got through a lot of chairs and trousers and you absolutely CANNOT make him laugh if he is sitting on the posh sofa in the *fancy room*.

Anyway, we lifted the car, had dinner and it was actually really nice to see **Grandma** and **Gramps** and I was almost slightly glad we had moved near them UNTIL . . .

. . . The whole way home **RED** just went on and on and ooooooooon about her new class and her new friends and being voted on to school council and how she has a special badge and gets to eat biscuits at the meetings. It was so totally annoying that if I hadn't been so completely exhausted I would have *zoomed* through the roof of the car to get away from her. Instead I imagined she was stranded in a laser cage on a planet that is so, so, sooooooo far away it doesn't even have a name yet. Which helped.

All of that is just typical of **RED** though . . . while I'm trailing around after **Serena** and **The Populars** with no friends and no votes and no badges and no biscuits, she has managed to completely fit in at school in no time and she doesn't even have to try.

When we FINALLY got home I went to see Bernard and after a brief chat we decided that tomorrow EVERYTHING will change and I WILL find some actual friends and I WILL get voted to be something and I WILL be a complete success **AND I WILL** have free biscuits. Probably. Bernard the guinea pig squeaked her approval and we both went to bed.

ZZZzzzzzzzz.

3

The bit where it doesn't go at all as planned...

Well, maybe EVERYTHING hasn't exactly changed yet, as I had planned. I still don't have real friends and I am not quite a complete success yet. Actually, I haven't even had a biscuit, free or otherwise. BUT I have put my name down to be school councillor for my class. I think this is a solid step in the RIGHT direction. If RED can do it then I am practically certain I can too, and there were only two other names on the list. One was *Sarah Wotton*, who is a complete know-it-all-teacher's-pet-snitch-pants, and the other was RiCKy OWeNS. I don't believe for one second that he put his own name down as he is rarely even in class and when he is, he is not listening. He would definitely not be a good person to represent the needs and concerns of Elephant Class. However, I am an actual superhero so maybe I might be able to do it? Maybe even be super at it?

I phoned **Tom** about it when I got home and he agrees – school councillor is pretty much in the bag.

BUT THEN . . .

I am not school councillor.

I came third.

SIGH

ARGH! What a day. Possibly the worst day EVER and I am no stranger to bad days – take the day I was thrown into an alien snot pit, or the day I was almost squeezed to death by an intergalactic slime worm. And this day definitely was WORSE . . .

Firstly, *Sarah Wotton* got her school councillor badge. She would not stop going on about it. And the biscuits. Apparently they are really delicious. Whatever.

Secondly, I found I still had gunk in my eyebrows in lesson three. I found this out by Barry Johnson shouting out very loudly that I had 'bogey eyebrows'.

Thirdly, **Serena** asked **Mrs Harris**, in front of the WHOLE class, if she could not be my buddy any more as she had been my buddy for AAAAGES and surely I knew where everything was by now.

While I do not have anything in common with **Serena** and **The Populars** and have felt boilingly uncomfortable trailing around after them, at least having her as my buddy gave me a place to be. Without her I will have to wander around on my own AND have to think about where I am wandering, which will be exhausting. And while I agree that **Serena** and I will never actually be for real buddies, when she asked **Mrs Harris** if we could unbuddy, well, I haven't felt that embarrassed since I was hit on the head with a **LLAMA** (it's a long story). It is one thing to know that you have no friends at school and probably never will, but it's quite a bit worse to have that confirmed in front of the WHOLE CLASS. *Sarah Wotton* even looked sad for me.

UGH.

Fourthly, **Mrs Harris** obviously thought that because I put my name down for school councillor I actually wanted to do something good for the school instead of just trying to compete with my irritating little sister. Er, actually, **Mrs Harris**, I do plenty of good things for people all the time – like SAVE THE WORLD. But **Mrs Harris** clearly decided this was not enough world-saving for one person and has made me **eco monitor** for our class. I don't even get a badge, just a ribbon. A green ribbon. And no biscuits. MMMMM'K.

I tried to talk to **Mrs Harris** about not being **eco monitor**. My old teacher, Mr Watson, would have known I already save the planet ALL THE TIME. I mean, can't someone else save the planet for a change, please? I explained all this to **Mrs Harris**, but she just smiled and said that I could use all my planet-saving experience for the job and to give it a go. Then she smiled in a way that told me we would not be discussing it any more.

ELEPHANT CLASS

ECO MONITOR

O I THE WAY HOME . . .

Despite flying to Pluto to let off some steam, I still felt completely wriggly and fully fed up when I got home. I decided I wouldn't actually tell anyone what was wrong because if they really cared they would just know, and gently lure it out of me with hot chocolate and sympathetic looks and pizza. So I went straight to my room and shut the door and decided I would stay there, in my room, on my own, until someone bothered to find out that my life was **RUBBISH**.

After about fifty hours, **WANDA** came into my room. I didn't think it was because she wanted to gently lure my problems out of me with snacks. **WANDA** confirmed my suspicions by sitting in the middle of my room, sniffing her foot and then telling me to be ready in one minute as **TWERKNADO** was about to **TWERK A TORNADO!**

Obviously. This was extra annoying as I was rather enjoying my misery and had just got halfway through painting my nails black to show everyone how unhappy I was . . .

Sometimes I wonder why I am not even a little bit popular. I mean, I save the planet and I can fly and I think I have good hair.

Oh, yes, AND I am *eco monitor*. Oh, well, I guess nobody's perfect. Who knows? Maybe that might even count for something? HAHAHAHAHAAAAA.

4

The bit where I decide
to use my eco powers
for good...

SUPERHERO STATIONERY!

Well, being **eco monitor** has multiplied the number of people I have spoken to at this school by at least 102 because it turned out there were a LOT of people in my school who all had something to say about how to save the planet. So I figured if I HAD to be **eco monitor** I may as well get a nice notebook out of it and write down everyone's suggestions in it. Mostly because my memory is RUBBISH – I think it was irreparably damaged that time I got hit by a **LLAMA** (long story). And also because everybody knows that whether you're superhero-saving the planet or just plain old saving the planet, stationery is KEY.

EVIL-DOINGS HIGHLIGHTERS

MISSION ACCOMPLISHED STAMP (OBVS!)

MISSION ACCOMPLISHED

GOOD AND EVIL DIVIDERS

DAMAGE LIMITATION SUPER GLUE

SUPER

This meant I had to tell **Mum** everything that had happened when she met us from school. It wasn't quite how I wanted her to find out about the millions of things that had been going wrong for me – it really didn't have any of the drama of my original plan (which was to sulk and look sad until I was gently encouraged to talk about it), but I didn't have time for all that now. I needed her to stop at Pilkingtons on the way home and get my notebook, because although I am allowed to fly to outer space to defeat evil baddies I am not allowed to get the bus into town on my own. **AMAZING**.

I was a bit irritated by this missed opportunity for some sympathy snacks, but the thing that REALLY annoyed me was RED being all pleased for me and saying how I would be the BEST eco monitor EVER and what a GREAT idea the notebook was and being so super enthusiastic. I don't know why exactly but it was sooooooo INFURIATING.

Anyway, we did stop at Pilkingtons and I got my eco notebook (green and recycled paper, obvs) and RED got a red one. She is super bright and of course completely AWESOME, but has ZERO imagination.

ZERO.

GREEN

When I called **Tom** and **Susie** that evening (they were doing homework together at **Susie**'s because it was Wednesday and we always did homework at **Susie**'s on Wednesdays) I tried not to moan too much about the whole **eco monitor** thing as I realised that moaning was all I had done in every single conversation I'd had with them since I left. Like **RED**, they were also really pleased and super enthusiastic about all of it. Unlike **RED**, it wasn't at all annoying when they said it. Hmmmmmm. I started to wonder whether maybe the whole **eco monitor** thing might NOT be the absolute worst thing in the world. Maybe.

THEN SUDDENLY...

. . . Right at the end of the week a girl from my class called Ivy came over with a suggestion. I mean, she would have an eco suggestion, wouldn't she? She's named after a plant. She told me that some BIG business-type people wanted to **bulldoze** the park next to school to build a car park! She thought that was a VERY bad idea because the trees were actually hundreds and hundreds of years old, and lots of birds and animals lived in the park and it was an extremely pretty and special place right next to school, and there were loads of car parks already and why on earth did we need any more and shouldn't we be cycling and walking more ANYWAY?

Then she finished by shoving a newspaper article into my hand which explained the whole thing.

She said all of this in a voice that made it sound like it was ALLLLL my fault, which I felt was pretty unfair, but when Ivy told me she had actually WANTED to be eco monitor, it made more sense. Apparently she had run the school allotment, successfully campaigned for exercise books made from recycled paper and organised a car-share rota for the whole of year two. Then she asked what qualifications was I bringing to the role?

I sort of had to laugh here because she clearly had never heard of my amazing track record for defeating baddies and therefore saving the planet LITERALLY ALL THE TIME!!! Ivy said, well, that's handy and I guess saving a park should be no problem then should it, and I said, huh, easy peasy lemon squeezy, and she said, great, then turned around and walked away. And THAT is how I decided what my first job as **eco monitor** would be.

I'd show **Ivy** who was saving the world around here. And while I was at it I could show **RED** and **Mum** and **Dad** and **WANDA** and EVERYONE that although some people might be school councillors, I – **eco monitor** – was the real mover and shaker around here. Ribbons might even become cooler than badges. I would save the park and everyone would think I was AWESOME!

All I had to do was work out how . . .

FIVE MINUTES LATER...

. . . I had thought and thought and thought and thought and still had no ideas so I decided to do what I always do when a mission is a bit tricky:

ASK **WANDA** . . .

WANDA licked my ear, sniffed the carpet and then told me that she wasn't authorised to help me with this mission, but she did, however, have a proper super mission from **MISSION CONTROL** and it was very urgent. Apparently uber-baddie **GooGoo** was having a particularly massive temper tantrum at COT2000 – his hilltop hideaway – and was threatening to fire all his toys out of PRAM1, his super high tech tank, onto a small neighbouring city, causing devastation, destruction and a right old mess.

None of this helped me with saving the park at all, in fact the complete opposite, and I started to tell **WANDA** this . . . but then I looked down and realised she had gone to find the others.

PIZAZZ AND RED DRAGON MEET AUNTY BLAZE, PHEW! BUT HOW WILL THEY STOP GOOGOO BREAKING THE EGG?

AS GOOGOO OPENS FIRE WITH A ROUND OF BOUNCY BALLS, OUR HEROES DIP, DUCK AND DIVE, SENDING THE BALLS FLYING AWAY FROM THE PRECIOUS EGG.

OH NO! NOW GOOGOO FIRES A ROUND OF CUDDLY TOYS...BUT, WELL, THEY ARE JUST TOO CUDDLY.

FINALLY GOOGOO FIRES A ROUND OF HIS BESTEST BUILDING BLOCKS... NO PROBLEM. BLOCKS STACKED, DANGER AVERTED.

AND THAT'S WHEN GOOGOO THREW THE BIGGEST TANTRUM. EVER.

ONCE GOOGOO HAD CALMED DOWN AUNTY BLAZE SENT HIM TO THE NAUGHTY STEP FOR A JOLLY GOOD THINK AND FANCY TOWN IS SAFE ONCE MORE. HOORAY!

AFTER...

It was so good to see **Aunty Blaze**. I think if I had to be anyone in the whole superhero world it would be **Aunty Blaze** for these reasons:

Aunty Blaze

She has a good name.

She doesn't have a cape.

She takes no nonsense from anyone, and would not in any way be bothered by **The Populars**.

She's completely awesome and fearless.

Her super power isn't embarrassing.

Her costume is actually quite cool.

She's always got a plan.

So it made perfect sense to ask **Aunty Blaze** how she would save the park next to school . . .

. . . **Mum** butted in and said that while that was the sort of thing we did to baddies on **OFFICIAL SUPERHERO MISSIONS** that wasn't how it worked normally – in the normal world – like the one most of us live in . . . most of the time. And THIS is exactly the sort of thing **Mum** would say. Yawn. I think she says things like that because **Aunty Blaze** is so successfully super. She's really high up at **MISSION CONTROL** in the **SUPER SECRET** department and has a really cool motorbike and 'lives life on her terms'. **Mum** even has to do all her washing she's so successfully super. And cook most of her meals.

Anyway, then **Mum** did the eyebrow waggling at **Aunty Blaze**, the thing grownups do at each other which means, 'SHHHHHH, this child will do everything you say'. **Aunty Blaze** then did the, 'Oh, right, OK, I'll shut up' face back at **Mum**. And they think we don't notice! FYI, grown-ups – kids are not stupid.

Mainly.

And while all of this was GREAT, I still had no plan. So I showed them both the article in the newspaper that Ivy gave me and explained VERY CLEARLY that these business types were going to hurt the planet by bulldozing a park to build another car park, which would mean more cars, which would hurt the planet even more, and surely that made them big bad baddies and wasn't the whole point of us, **SUPERHEROES**, to defeat the baddies however we needed to?

And Aunty Blaze said, 'EXACTLY,' then pulled the 'Oh, right, OK, I'll shut up' face again when Mum glared at her.

Mum said, well, no, bulldozing a park did not seem like a very nice thing to do at all but that the council was probably going to give them permission and that meant you couldn't just barge in and smush their bulldozers, however much you might like to. Because superhero or not, you would probably end up in jail. And Aunty Blaze said I should listen to my mother.

At this point I thought my head might actually explode. I asked **Mum** and ~~Aunty Blaze~~ what was the point of being *SUPER* and saving the stupid world the WHOLE time if the world just kept hurting itself anyway? Amazingly **Mum** said she actually agreed with me and she thought about it all the time, BUT we all had to remember that superheroes did lots of good things and we had to keep doing good things and hope lots of other people would do good things too so actually all the good things would outweigh the bad things. She suggested that maybe a good place to start was to talk to the BIG business types, because that is how lots of differences are settled and blah blah blah.

SUDDENLY...

Then **RED** backflipped into the room and *blew* the perfect ~~fireball~~ and told us she wasn't school councillor any more, she was now **CHIEF** school councillor.

5

The bit where it all goes wrong...

THE NEXT DAY...

I told **Ivy** that my **mum** had suggested we go to the **BIG** business type's offices and just have a nice chat about it. I only said this because I had nothing better to suggest, but surprisingly **Ivy** agreed and thought that maybe if we pointed out how silly the car park idea was they would see sense. We could just remind them that we do **NOT** need more cars but we do need more trees.

Also we could take along some **doughnuts** because they always help things along. I was not at all sure about this plan as it lacked all the whizzy superhero/world-saving things I am used to, but I DO like doughnuts, so it was decided we would visit the offices of **CASHCORP** after school.

BUT THEN...

I am not entirely sure how it could have gone worse and I didn't even get a sniff of a **doughnut**. It turns out the **BIG CHEESE** at **CASHCORP** was in actual fact *Serena* from **The Populars**'s dad, **Mr Piffle!**

Once we finally got to see him (a very long story involving a few white lies about a school paper, a smidge of flying and tiny bit of sneakiness) we were both a bit frazzled, and in actual fact he doesn't even like **doughnuts** so they were no help.

Really. Who doesn't like **doughnuts**?

Anyway, standing in front of him and all of his MEDIUM TO **LARGE CHEESES** was even more scary than **DABOMB**'s robot army. At least you know where you stand with a robot army, i.e. they all want to **ZAP** you with their *LASER EYES*. I had no idea what these **CHEESES** were thinking.

As I'm *eco monitor* and therefore in charge, I made **Ivy** do all the talking. And while **Ivy**'s speech was really very informative and she put across a good argument, it didn't really seem to be grabbing the attention of all the different-sized **cheeses**. It felt like it was missing all the *whizziness* of my previous planet-saving, more superhero-type missions so, quite surprisingly for me, I decided to take ACTION.

Not content with telling us off in person, **Serena**'s dad told on us to **Mrs Harris** too, which seemed a bit of an overreaction. I mean, it's not like anyone ended up covered in ~~radioactive slime~~ or anything. So then **Mrs Harris** told us off as well. Well, sort of, I mean, she told us we probably shouldn't have gone to **CASHCORP**'s offices and made such a mess and I most likely should not have called **Serena**'s dad a NITWIT. But **Mrs Harris** was smiling the whole time and **Ivy** and I left feeling very confused as to whether we were actually in trouble or not.

I started to feel that I was making a proper mess of being **eco monitor**. If I am honest, after all my world-saving and facing deadly villains and *zooming* through outer space, I thought saving a park would be a breeze. But it turns out that when your baddies are dressed in suits and they don't use *LASERS* but bits of paper and suitcases, they are much, much harder to defeat.

Serena obviously heard all about it from her **BIG CHEESE** dad and decided to bring it up in tutor time in front of the WHOLE CLASS, focusing mainly on the tea trolley incident (I only nudged it) and not so much on the bit where I did a perfect somersault over the board table, or even when **Ivy** gave her very good speech. Of course nobody bothered to stop to think about who was actually trying to save the planet and who was being a meany, instead they all just laughed along with **Serena**'s very one-sided and completely inaccurate retelling of our 'meeting'.

Sometimes it seems that the less you actually do, the more people think you're great. Take **Serena**, for example. I have to spend my leisure time saving the world for HER. Well, not just for her, obviously, but still I am running and flying around averting certain doom all over the place and what is she doing? NOTHING. But none of that matters because everyone thinks **Serena** is great and I am a loser.

IT'S SOOOOOO

OO UNFAIR...

And why does no one even appreciate how great MY hair is? I mean it is, isn't it?

6

The bit where it
all goes wrong
AGAIN...

It just felt like this park-saving was much harder than it should be. I was supposed to be good at this **world-saving** business. It's not like I would ever be able to rely on long division as a fallback, and I'm useless at netball (I think both are related to the time I got hit on the head with a **LLAMA** – long story), so if I wasn't able to save a teeny bit of green space, what was the point of me? Maybe I just

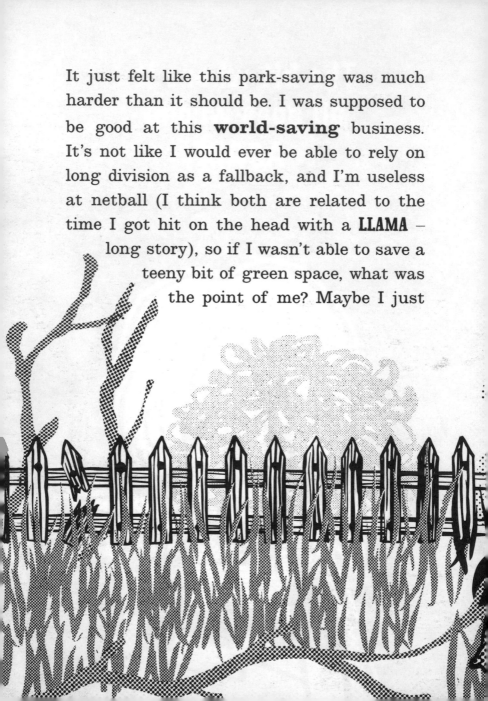

hadn't been super ENOUGH at the meeting. MAYBE it was time to take a bit of ~~Aunty Blaze~~'s advice and go all-out **SUPER**.

If I was SUPER careful **Mum** would never even have to know.

MY GENIUS PLAN TO SAVE THE DAY...

IF THERE ARE NO DIGGERS AND BULLDOZERS THEN CASHCORP CAN'T DIG AND FLATTEN THE PARK. SIMPLE!

SO...I ZOOMED OVER TO CASHCORP JUST TO BORROW THE DIGGERS AND BULLDOZERS...

...AND PUT THEM IN A SAFE PLACE LIKE PLUTO.

AND HOW DID I DO THAT?

WELL, WITH MY SUPER POWER, WHICH IS FAAAAAAR TOO EMBARRASSING, SO I AM AFRAID YOU CAN'T SEE THAT BIT.

Yes, it's true. Even superheroes get grounded, and I was most certainly grounded. Literally. I wasn't allowed to fly for a week.

Everyone was furious with me, even Ivy. She said something about it making US look like the baddies rather than **CASHCORP**. This obviously being the exact opposite of what we wanted.

So I had got myself in MASSIVE trouble, been grounded, made the only person at school who talks to me FURIOUS and not helped save the park AT ALL.

Of course **Serena** had something to say about it, too. Right in front of everyone, at home time, she made a big thing about how I was just a typical super, *zooming* about making a mess of EVERYTHING, and how I shouldn't be allowed to meddle and . . .

. . . But she didn't get to say anything else because that's when RED stepped in. I don't think I have ever been more pleased to see RED (or actually ever pleased to see her) and it didn't even occur to me to be irritated that my BABY sister had saved me from **Serena**. Then she gave me a super-speedy piggyback all the way home.

I called **Susie** and told her I had decided I would resign as *eco monitor* the next morning. **Ivy** would obviously be much better than me. I was clearly no good at being NORMAL and possibly not very good at being **SUPER**. **Susie** said she thought I was actually pretty good at being normal and even really great at being **SUPER**, but just in case we had a quick brainstorm about what other options I had.

Then **WANDA** padded into my room (without even knocking), rolled around on my homework, knocked over my drink, told me to get off the phone and come to the kitchen for an **urgent briefing**.

When I got to the kitchen **RED** gave me one of those 'I'm just SO sorry for you' smiles and it did occur to me to be irritated by my BABY sister.

FACT: those smiles do not help anything and only make you feel cross on top of whatever it is they are sorry about. UGH.

WANDA told us that **CAPTAIN CHAOS** and **STAR SLAYER** were causing a right old commotion in the outer reaches of the galaxy and we needed to go and see exactly what they were up to and SHUT. IT. DOWN.

This was a HUGE relief as I had been getting worried about having to be super again after the **Mr Piffle** debacle and although **CAPTAIN CHAOS** and **STAR SLAYER** sound scary (and to be fair they quite often are) they are also **KAPOW**'s mum and dad. I have known **KAPOW** my WHOLE life, almost. We met at nursery and hit it off straight away. And even when we realised that he is a super villain and I am a superhero, we still stayed friends . . . . super secret friends.

HOW KAPOW AND PIZAZZ STAY SUPER SECRET FRIENDS...

AT NURSERY... NO NEED TO WAIT UNTIL SNACK TIME...

WHEN ONE OF YOU CAN FLY! YUM!

AT SCHOOL...NEED TO SHARE SOMETHING HILARIOUS

...NOT A PROBLEM WHEN ONE OF YOU HAS TELEPATHY AS A SUPER POWER. LOL

THE REST OF THE TIME...

I MEAN, YOU WOULD IF YOU COULD, WOULDN'T YOU?

EYE ROLL

IT TURNS OUT THAT KAPOW AND I BOTH FEEL THE SAME WAY ABOUT BEING SUPER. AS YOU KNOW, I AM REALLY NOT AT ALL SURE ABOUT BEING A SUPERHERO AND KAPOW IS NOT AT ALL KEEN ON BEING A SUPER VILLAIN. THIS MEANS THAT WHENEVER WE MEET UP TO FIGHT IT OUT, KAPOW AND I USUALLY JUST PRETEND WRESTLE THEN SNEAK OFF FOR A CHAT. **THIS MISSION WAS NO DIFFERENT . . .**

The bit where Gramps gives us a GOOD IDEA

THE NEXT DAY...

First thing, I asked Ivy what she thought we should do to save the park. I got a very strong feeling Ivy had been preparing for this moment, which made me feel even worse for not asking sooner.

Ivy thought we should organise a few of us to hold a protest by the entrance to the park after school on Friday. So when all the parents came to collect their children from school they could see what was going on and then they would want to save the park too.

While I thought this seemed like a NICE idea, it didn't really feel like it had any of the punch of our first two tries. How would standing around and just chatting to people save anything? I started to say as much to **Ivy**, but then I remembered **KAPOW**'s EYE ROLL and how my attempts at park-saving had worked out and so instead of telling **Ivy** her idea was pants, I asked if she wanted to come round for tea so we could make a plan for Friday.

And amazingly she said yes!

School seemed to go on for ever and **Serena** really didn't miss a single chance to tease me allll day . . .

AT BREAK

IN CLASS

AT LUNCH

EVEN DURING PE!

. . . But by the end of the day I had sort of zoned out and couldn't really hear her any more. It's a survival trick I learned from living with RED and her going on and on and on and on about EVERYTHING,

ALL

THE

TIME.

The bell for home time went and I met Ivy at the school gates. We walked home because I was still grounded (for anything other than planetary emergencies) and Ivy can't fly, obviously, so it took aaaages, but it did give us a chance to chat about our **park protest**. We made up a sort of songy chant thing we could sing to get people's attention. I had never had to sing/chant to save the planet before and I wondered if maybe this could be my signature **SUPERHERO** move – instead of my completely embarrassing, humiliating one that I still don't want to talk about. Then Ivy asked what we would have for tea and I think she was a bit disappointed when I said spaghetti. I am not sure what she thought supers ate, but she was obviously hoping for something more exciting than spaghetti.

I wish!

When we got home we told **Mum** all about our idea and she said it sounded great and that we should probably go and speak to **Gramps** because he had done a little bit of protesting himself back in the day.

So we did. **Mum** even drove us over while **Dad** cooked tea. **Gramps** and **Grandma** were very pleased to see us and **Grandma** asked if I had explained the not-making-**Gramps**-laugh rule to **Ivy** and I hadn't so I did, but this made **Ivy** laugh, which made **Gramps** laugh, which made all of us laugh and this made **Gramps** laugh even more and before you knew it, he trumped, and **Grandma** was putting out a flaming scatter cushion with her handy handbag-size fire extinguisher.

We decided to go outside and walk around the garden in case of any more little 'fireballs', and **Gramps** told us all about his protest. Apparently, an **ANGRY SHOUTY MAN** started telling anyone who would listen that supers were different and not like normal people, which is sort of true, but then he said that's why they couldn't be trusted as they would only use their **SUPER** powers for themselves. And because of that he said supers should go and live far away from everyone else and STAY AWAY. And some people started to listen to him because, well, he was angrily shouting

VERY
LOUDLY.

Obviously **Gramps** didn't agree with what the **ANGRY SHOUTY MAN** was saying for lots of reasons – the main one being that supers were only being super to protect **EVERYONE IN THE WHOLE WORLD, EVEN THE WHOLE UNIVERSE** and, actually, they were much more like normal people than they were different from them. They could just fly and stuff too.

Firstly, it made **Gramps** cross (which I could NOT imagine) and he wanted to whizz around the planet a million times to turn back time and stop the **ANGRY SHOUTY MAN** before he started shouting or even got angry. Then he thought he might like to push the **ANGRY SHOUTY MAN** into deepest space so the man could see how he liked it out on his own, but then **Gramps** finally calmed down and realised that these ideas were not very nice at all and that using his **SUPER** powers to try and solve this problem would only make things worse.

People would only see how different he was from them, not how he was the same, and that was exactly what the **ANGRY SHOUTY MAN** wanted. **Gramps** realised he could only really fix this problem by being everyday super. Not *SUPER* super. So he went to the garage and used some old wood and a stick (which he thought must have been left there by the people who lived there before because he did NOT do DIY) and he used them to make a sign, then off he went to where the **ANGRY SHOUTY MAN** was angrily shouting and he started to calmly protest. He even made up a song too.

It turned out lots of other people agreed with **Gramps** and some of them joined in. First it was mainly other supers, but slowly all kinds of people got involved. And the more people got involved, the more people noticed and eventually the **ANGRY SHOUTY MAN** couldn't shout above everyone else's singing, so he shut up and went away (even though no one had told him to).

So that was that. Well, until the next time, **Gramps** said.

Then **Gramps** took me and **Ivy** to the garage where there was lots of old wood and sticks (because when he made that first sign he realised he actually LOVED DIY) and we made some signs for our park protest. It felt totally weird not to just *whizz* off and use my embarrassing super power to save the day, but instead I got to hang out with **Gramps** and **Ivy** in the garage, chatting and painting and hammering. I wondered if this really could actually make a difference and I wasn't at all sure it could, as it was all just too, well, normal, but it was also very nice so I did it anyway. Ivy said the signs looked really good and **Gramps** seemed very pleased about this and said he couldn't be happier as he'd thought his planet-saving days were over. Then **Grandma** brought us all some crisps and biscuits and I thought how much nicer other planet-saving missions would be if they involved more **snacks**.

At school the next day Ivy and I drew some leaflets to hand out at the protest and we photocopied them in the library. (Mr Simpson, the librarian, thought it was a great idea as he ate his lunch in the park every day AND he said he would come along on Friday to support the protest.)

SAVE OUR PARK!!!

Our lovely park is UNDER THREAT!

We want parks NOT CARS!!!

Please come and help us save our park.

WHEN? This Friday, after school.

WHERE? THE PARK (next to school)

WHY? Because it is lovely and there are lots of animals living there and it belongs to US!!!

The bit before it all kicks off

THE BIG DAY ARRIVED ...

I woke up on Friday with *BUBBLES* in my tummy and this was extremely weird as all I was going to do was stand about with a sign. It's not like I had to f1y off into deepest **darkest** space to stop an alien overlord or anything. All my lessons took forever, and *Ivy* and I could barely eat any lunch at all. I think her tummy had *BUBBLES* too. And then ALL OF A SUDDEN it was home time ...

Gramps was outside school with the signs as we had arranged, and we picked them up, stood by the park and started our chant. It all felt a bit silly at first, just me, *Ivy* and

Gramps chanting away, and people trying
to chat over the top. I felt like I should DO
something **SUPER** to get things moving. But
then I remembered where that had got me
before, and I really did want to save the park
this time, so I just kept going.

Molly and Ed, Ivy's friends, met us and joined in, then the librarian, Mr Simpson, came along and then even Mrs Harris. Serena looked at us like we smelled funny and started calling someone on the phone that she is absolutely not allowed to take to school.

RED brought the school council along and I thought, UGH, TYPICAL, I can't even have a protest without her butting in. But then they all set up a **LEMONADE** stall just by the entrance to the park, and people actually seemed to like that a lot and even took their **LEMONADE** into the park and it felt like although nothing was really happening, something was sort of happening and that something was hopefully a good thing.

We handed out our leaflets. Molly had even started a petition for people to sign. And they did! We kept singing and chanting and waving our signs about. Then **Mum** came down with **Grandma** and **WANDA**, and I thought how nice that was until it was actually completely awful because right in the middle of our protest, **WANDA** piped up with an **URGENT MISSION**. I looked at **Mum**, who just shrugged her shoulders and did the 'I'm sorry' smile, which still didn't help. I thought Ivy would hate me because just like always, right in the middle of the best thing I have done in ages, I had to *zoom off* for a mission. And it was gross **big baddie MEGAVOM** and those **missions never ended well.**

GUYS? GUYS? GUYS!!!

PUKEY VILLAIN MEGAVOM IS ABOUT TO THROW UP ALL OVER A SMALL PRINCIPALIT YOU MUST SAVE THEM FROM THIS HURLIN HORROF

MEGAVOM WAS ON TOP OF THE HIGHEST HILL IN THE TINY PRINCIPALITY. AND HE WAS ALMOST READY TO BLOW...

HEAVE

CHUNKS...

AS OUR **HEROES** FLEW IN THEY COULD SEE THEY HAD NO TIME TO SPARE...

BLARF!

...ONE OF THEM WOULD HAVE TO DISTRACT MEGAVOM...
BUT WHO...

YEP. I GOT THE SHORT STRAW.

HURL

SPLAT

DRIP DRIP

AND THANKS TO OUR BRAVE (SLIGHTLY PUKEY) HERO,

MEGAVOM WAS FOILED ONCE AGAIN.

ROOOOAAR!!!

RUMBLE!   RUMBLE!

I *zoomed* back to the park as fast as I could, which fortunately *whizzed* most of the puke off me, but I still landed in a panic. I needn't have though, because **Gramps** and **Ivy** were laughing (but not quite enough for a fireball – phew) and everything seemed OK. **Ivy** said they had held the fort just fine, and there was even a whisper going about that the local newspaper was going to come along. Oh, and the school council had run out of **LEMONADE** and wasn't it great that people seemed to actually care about this little park after all and . . .

Well, I'll never know what she was going to say next because I couldn't hear **Ivy** over the **ROAR** of a bulldozer. And the **ROAR** of **Mr Piffle** on the bulldozer.

The action-packed bit

(where I have to use my stupid super power)

Mr Piffle *zoomed* ^{up} to the park. Well, I say *zoomed* – bulldozers don't actually go that fast so it took him quite a while and it was a bit embarrassing, but when he did make it to the park entrance he was LIVID and a sort of purply colour.

Purple **Mr Piffle** stopped the bulldozer because it was really quite hard to hear him over the top of the racket it was making, then he looked down on us and told us we were all standing in the way of progress, literally. We should stop being silly because of course we needed more space to park more cars and what was the point of a tiny, scruffy park anyway? And we should not concern ourselves with the business of **BIG** business and we should just let the **BIG** businessmen get on with it because after all they knew what was best and we should also GET OUT OF THE WAAAAAY.

Then Ivy did something extremely brave and stepped forward and very politely and not at all shoutily, she pointed out to Mr Piffle that people were enjoying their little park and why would he want to take that away and, anyway, just how much money were he and CASHCORP going to make out of squishing our park and building their car park? Amazingly, Mr Piffle went even more purple and managed to look even more angry, which I did not believe was possible until I saw him do it. If he was SUPER that would for sure be his SUPER power.

ANGRY HAIR FLICK

LIVID EYEBROW WAGGLING

IRATE EAR BRISTLE

EXTRA FUMING NOSTRIL FLARE

FURIOUS EAR FLAPPING

RAGING SPITTLE

PURPLEY FACE X 100

Mr Piffle started up his bulldozer again and headed towards the park entrance. I was quite sure all the briefcases and bits of paper in the world did not mean he could just drive through our protest and squash the park without proper permission or anything. Everyone sort of panicked a bit and **Ivy** looked really sad. It seemed such a shame that just as everyone realised how much they liked the little park, **Mr Piffle** was going to squash it anyway. We had to stop him. But how?

I looked at **Mum**, who nodded and mouthed, 'Go ON!' (I mean, she might have actually said it but the bulldozer made it impossible to tell), then I looked at **WANDA**, who sniffed a flower, scratched her ear and nodded too. Even **Gramps** gave me a shove. And then I looked at Ivy. I had messed things up so many times trying to be *SUPER*, and I wanted to make a friend as well as save the little park, but Ivy just looked so sad and I knew I had to do something. The most embarrassing thing, the thing I tried so hard all the time NOT to do. But here I was about to do it in front of EVERYONE at school, slightly covered in vomit . . .

I would have to use my *SUPER POWER*.

SLOWLY, A GLITTER STORM APPEARED IN FRONT OF ME AND I USED THAT GLITTER STORM (I CAN CONTROL IT WITH MY JAZZ HANDS – I KNOW!) TO PUSH THE BULLDOZER BACK ON TO THE ROAD AND AWAY FROM THE LITTLE PARK.

Well, this made **Mr Piffle** properly angry and he jumped down from his now very sparkly bulldozer and started yelling right in the protesters' faces. All this happened just as the local paper turned up and took lots of photos of him **screaming**. This seemed to make him even more angry and then everyone started booing and **Serena** and **The Populars** disappeared and **Mr Piffle** looked extremely bothered, made a very strange angry gargling noise and stomped off, leaving his **DISCO** bulldozer right in the middle of the road! I used my jazz hands/glitter storm and carefully moved it to the side of the road so everyone could go home. (I mean, everyone had seen my embarrassing **SUPER POWER** at this point so WHATEVER.) But then the best thing happened. No one (well, almost no one) went home. Everyone cheered and stayed in the park and **RED** used her super speed to whip up some more **LEMONADE** and then the ice-cream van turned up and it was really, **REALLY** super.

10

The end bit . . .

. . . or is it?

Yes . . .

. . . or is it?

It turned out that because **Mr Piffle** hadn't got permission yet to squish the park, he was now in BIG TROUBLE and **Serena** was extremely quiet about that, but she was less quiet about my embarrassing **SUPER POWER** and teases me about it whenever she can.

But do you know what? I don't even mind that much because now I have a friend at school, one who actually thinks my **SUPER POWER** is pretty cool. I KNOW! In fact, I have three friends – **Ivy**, **Molly** and **Ed**, or the eco council, as we are otherwise known. We hold regular council meetings in the park and **Tom** and **Susie** even came along to one

of them. Well, it was more of a picnic than
a meeting, but it was great all the same.
And as I looked around at our slightly less-
scruffy-looking park (**Gramps** now heads up
a volunteer group who are making it pretty
special – I guess **he just can't stop saving
the planet!**) I realised that no matter how
much I might not want to ALWAYS save the
planet (and sometimes it seems like there is
just too much to do), I am always glad when
I have. One bit at a time. So far we haven't
had to protest again, but **Gramps** said the
garage is ready if we do.

And now you know. That's my **SUPER SUPER POWER**. Not Kung Fu, not *LASER EYES*, not even supersonic projectile vomiting. No, my **SUPER POWER** is **jazz hands**. Jazz hands that then create a glitter* storm that I can move at my will. And, yes, it is COMPLETELY EMBARRASSING.

* biodegradable, obviously!

TA-DAH

I guess now you know
why I am called
Pizazz.

TO BE CONTINUED . . .

Look out for
Pizazz's
next SUPER
adventure!

ALSO every month we will be giving 100 (yes, that's 100) people the chance to win a PIZAZZ SUPER CLUB KIT, full of PIZAZZ merchandise! All you have to do is enter the free prize draw* and keep your fingers crossed!

IT'S NOT EASY BEING SUPER...

* this is the T&Cs bit: To enter you must be 18 or over — so you'll have to get an adult to do it for you. Full T&Cs can be found on pizazzsuperclub.co.uk